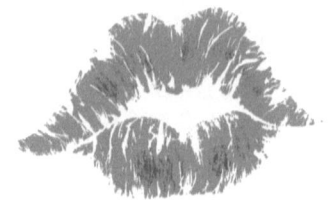

EVERNIGHT PUBLISHING ®

www.evernightpublishing.com

SAM CRESCENT

Copyright© 2021

Sam Crescent

Editor: Karyn White

Cover Art: Sour Cherry Designs

Jacket Design: Jay Aheer

ISBN: 978-0-3695-0329-9

DEVIL'S PROMISE

DEDICATION

To all of my Devil fans out there who can't get enough,
this is for you.

DEVIL'S PROMISE

DEVIL'S PROMISE

Chaos Bleeds, 12

Sam Crescent

Copyright © 2018

Chapter One

"Judi and Ripper will take care of the kids. Simon's gone to Fort Wills. It'll just be the two of us," Devil said.

"Are you feeling bad because you missed our anniversary, even though it wasn't technically our anniversary?" Lexie asked, hands on her full hips. "It's just the day *I* consider our anniversary. The day we met."

Devil loved her body. Nothing had changed since the first time they met all those years ago, and even now he couldn't get enough of her. Staring at her, he wanted her. His cock was rock-hard, ready to be inside her.

"And I'm going to make it up to you."

"By taking me away to some exotic island for a few days?"

"I was thinking Vegas, but I can stretch to an exotic island." He was so pissed at himself for forgetting their "anniversary," as she'd declared every single year that it was important. That day had changed the rest of his life and made him decide to stick around in Piston County, not only to set down roots for the club but to be a husband to Lexie, a father to their children.

"What about the club? You're at a place right now where you can't just leave it."

"We're going to get away for a couple of days. Just you and me. There's not going to be anyone there to worry about."

He opened his legs and grabbed Lexie's hand, pulling her close. "I want to do something special for you, baby."

"I know, and I know that you have an obligation to the club. You don't have time to be running around."

"I have enough time."

"What about all this with Darcy?"

"It'll be waiting for us when we get back. We need this." He knew that if he didn't get Lexie away now, she'd be at Fort Wills helping out with Darcy whenever she could. He didn't have a problem with that. The Skulls were their family as well, but he also didn't want Lexie to tire herself out. With all of their kids and their own hectic lives, he knew Lexie always put herself last.

It's why he made sure to put her first, even before the whole of the club. He made sure she stayed well. When they were first married he lost count of the number of times he saw her curled up on the sofa, when she hadn't eaten but was passed out from exhaustion. That kind of shit would never happen on his watch. He wouldn't allow it, simple as that.

She sighed. "You know I don't like leaving the kids behind."

"I hate to break it to you, babe, but they're going to leave us soon. Have families of their own, fall in love. All that kind of shit. You don't even need to worry about them."

Lexie cupped his face, pressing her lips against his. "I don't know if I like you all the time."

"We'll always have each other, and that's what counts."

"You're going to let Simon go to Fort Wills with Tabitha?"

"No, he's actually staying with Anthony, which is far away from Tabitha."

She chuckled. "You do know if he's anything like his dad, he'll find a way to be with her."

Devil sighed. "They're still young. I won't worry until he knows how to use his dick."

"Seriously, I can't even begin to believe you're thinking like that right now."

He gripped her full ass. After all the kids they had, her body was still fucking perfect to him. Even with the stretch marks and fuller curves, he couldn't get enough of her.

"We've got a couple more months."

"More months? He's a teenager, Devil."

"So, it'll take a little longer for him to know what to do with it. He'll be playing with his dick for a long time."

"Ew, I can't think about this."

Lexie made to get off his lap, but he wouldn't let her go. "Woman, I've missed you, and I want you."

She rolled her eyes. "Does this have something to do with that picnic? I told you I don't care about what they have. It's never been about the money and stuff."

"It's not about them at all. It's about you and me and the fact we've not had any time alone in forever. It's been the kids or the fucking drama. I want out for a few days with you." He took her hand that held the wedding band he'd given her. "Just you and me."

"You'll leave your leather cut at home."

"No chance of that. You see, I want you to wear that cut while I fuck you again and again."

"Okay, well you better change your plans with Alex. I have no interest in going to Vegas."

"What if I ... called in a favor from one of the Billionaire boys?"

She chuckled. "You call in a favor?"

"Hell, yeah, they owe us."

She ran her hand down his body, cupping his cock. "You do whatever it is you feel you need to do. I'll always be here for you." She kissed his cheek. "It *has* been a long time since it has just been the two of us." Lexie pulled away, that sexy smile across her lips letting him know she was thinking of all the delicious, naughty things he could do to her. Damn, it was like he hadn't seen that look in her eyes in so long that he had to wonder if he imagined it.

Watching her bend down to grab the towel he'd dumped earlier, he groaned. She was doing this on purpose because she knew just how much he loved watching her ass.

"Just the two of us, no club, no kids, just us. I wonder what we could do together without any interruptions." She tilted her head to the side.

She left the room, and he pulled out his cell phone, dialing pussy boy, meaning Russ from the Billionaire Bikers MC.

He wasn't afraid to call in a few favors, especially as that biker needed a shitload from him in the coming months and weeks. Taking on an entire world of traffickers wasn't going to come easy. It just so happened, he hated those that abused women and was more than happy to bring them down.

****

"It'll be good for you and Devil to get away. I can't even remember the last time you did. You've always been pregnant," Judi said, picking up one of the shirts from the large pile that Lexie was folding.

"I don't mind. I love my family. Vacations with the family are great."

"Are you nervous about being alone with Devil?" Judi asked.

"No, of course not."

Judi chuckled. "How long has it been since you two had some real alone time?"

Lexie blew some hair out of her face and scrunched up her nose. "I can't ... no, I don't remember. We've always had the kids, and then of course there is always something going on at the club. We've got the store, and everything is crazy. You know that."

Judi was her stepdaughter, even though there were only a few years between them. She'd been a forced teenage prostitute that Devil had saved. Lexie had married Devil, and they'd adopted Judi as their own.

"You're worried. I can see it."

"I'm not worried. I just don't think it's the right time."

"What's the right time?" Simon asked, walking into the laundry room without a shirt on.

"Are we just forgoing clothes now as well?" Lexie asked.

"I'm out of shirts."

He walked to them and pulled one over. "What are we ladies gossiping about?"

Lexie laughed. Pulling him in for a hug, she kissed his head. "You're not a lady."

"Please, I can gossip like the best of them."

"Does Tabby know you like to go all lady?" Judi asked.

"Tabby knows everything," he said. "We don't have secrets."

"You don't?" Lexie asked.

"We're best friends. She's my girl. I've got no reason to keep secrets from her. Are you and Dad going away?"

"Nothing gets past you, does it?" Lexie asked.

"You totally should go, Mom. You deserve it."

She looked down at the laundry, feeling that twinge in her chest when he called her mom. He didn't know the truth, and Devil never wanted him to find out. Simon wasn't her son, but her sister Kayla's.

"What's wrong?" Simon asked.

"It's nothing."

"You really should go though."

"You're only saying that because Dad has agreed to let you go to Fort Wills," Judi said.

"Whatever. Shouldn't you be, like, a grown-up now? You're a married woman," Simon said.

"So, you're getting older and that still makes me your grown sister. I can totally tease you if I want."

He gave her the finger, and she burst out laughing.

"You're so cute."

"Simon, don't swear."

"Dad does it all the time."

"I know."

"I only used my fingers. I didn't actually speak."

"You're still swearing."

"Remember that year he swore all the time and at the end there was, like, three grand there?" Judi said.

Simon burst out laughing. "That was the best New Year's fireworks display ever."

"You keep swearing, and I'll make sure you start putting into the cuss jar, Simon."

He shrugged. "You really should go. It'll do you good." He finished folding up the washing with them and left.

"He's getting old so fast," she said.

"You need to stop looking guilty when he calls you Mom," Judi said.

She sighed. "Some days it's harder than others, you know."

"I do."

Judi moved round behind her. "I love you, Lex, always."

She hugged her close and sighed. "I'm going to deliver these clothes."

Lifting up the laundry basket, she made her way upstairs to the bedrooms. Devil had bought her the perfect place. Her life was everything she wanted it to be and more. He made sure she wanted for nothing, but right now, something made her nervous, and she didn't know what.

Putting the kids' clothes away, she finished with hers and Devil's. Her reflection caught her attention. She'd never been supermodel-thin or even slender. When Devil saw her, she'd been working the pole, stripping for money.

All those years later and kids, and her body was … different.

Her thighs were bigger, with marks of cellulite. No matter how many stomach exercises she did, there was still a pouch there, and of course her tits were huge with a little more hang.

She loved Devil with all of her heart.

But—and she hated this—what if it was only because of the kids and the club that they were still together?

Being around the other clubs at the picnic the

Billionaire Bikers MC hosted had made her realize how different she was. She wasn't young anymore, and her body wasn't that of a full-figured stripper.

She was a mom.

Pulling her shirt up over her head and her sweatpants down, she stared at herself. They had sex all the time, and when his arms were around her, she had no doubt. Since coming home though, she couldn't bring herself to be naked in front of him. Did he want someone younger? Someone who had a tighter body?

Tears flooded her eyes, and she quickly pulled her clothes back on. It was stupid of her to even think about this.

She went into the bathroom, putting the laundry basket down, and then walked downstairs toward the kitchen.

A picture of the two of them together with Simon in her arms caught her attention. It had been taken so long ago during the summer. Simon wore one of those cute summer baby hats with shorts and a plain blue t-shirt.

Devil had his arms around her with his chin resting on her shoulder, and she smiled at the camera.

Not once in all the years they'd been together had she ever doubted herself like this. She hated these feelings that were bubbling up inside her, but she couldn't stop them. What was worse, she had no one to talk to about it. There was Eva, Tiny's wife, but she wouldn't understand.

So, Lexie tried to ignore it, which was easy to do at home in Piston County. Alone, together, no distractions, it would be a lot harder to do.

Chapter Two

"You're seriously asking me this?" Russ asked.

Devil smiled as he worked on his bike. "Come on, you really didn't think you were going to ask for that huge-ass favor and then not get a call back?"

"Not this fucking huge."

"You're telling me one of you guys doesn't have a nice, big, fancy island where I can take my woman?"

He heard Russ sigh across the line and knew he'd won, not that he'd expected anything different. He would always win. That's what made him Devil, leader of the Chaos Bleeds.

Whatever he wanted, he got.

Right now, he needed some alone time with his woman because he knew something was up. It wasn't *just* that though. He wanted to spend some time with her. There'd been a little distance since they got back from the picnic, and he didn't like that.

Lexie was his, and he would get to the bottom of what was bugging her one way or the other.

"Yes, we do. Fine, fine. I'll get everything ready. Just give me the dates you need."

Devil told him the dates, and Russ promised to call him back.

Closing his cell phone, he placed it on the floor beside his bike. Russ would come through because if he didn't there would be fucking hell to pay. There's no question about it, Devil wouldn't accept no.

If he didn't do this now, then it would wait another year or another couple of years. Lexie always found something that kept her busy, and it had been too long since he had her on his own.

"You okay, Prez?" Pussy asked, coming to sit on the wall opposite the bike.

"Yeah, why wouldn't I be?"

"You've got this frown that screams you're going to kill someone. If it's going to be so much fun, I want in."

Devil shook his head. "No fighting. Just waiting for Russ."

"What are you calling that fucker for?"

He stared at Pussy. "For Lexie."

"I thought Alex was all over it."

"Lexie doesn't want to go to Vegas." He didn't want to go to fucking Vegas, either. The only reason he'd agreed was the free hotel. He didn't intend to actually leave the room, but Lexie, she was changing.

"There is that. Sasha loves Vegas, but then she's not getting over all the twinkling lights and the stuff she can see now."

"You sound troubled, friend."

"Not troubled at all. Just wondering what all this shit means with the Billionaires. You know?"

"It's not going to mean a whole lot of change."

"Yeah, it kind of will."

"We'll be back up or safe houses," Devil said. "I won't put my club in any more danger."

"I get that."

"You're worried."

"Nah, I'm fine. At times I forget that Sasha can see and I don't have to worry about everything." Pussy shrugged. "Not a whole lot I can change."

Devil wiped the grease from his hand as he looked at his friend. "Are you missing the fact she's not a hundred percent dependent on you?"

"No, of course not."

Pussy was lying.

Okay, it was time for him to do his Prez thing.

Moving beside Pussy, he saw the other man was

clearly pouting.

"You don't need to lie to me."

"I'm not one of those guys that needs a woman."

"Sasha's not just any woman. She's your wife and the mother of your child."

"It's fucking wrong is what it is," Pussy said.

"What is?"

"Feeling like this. I should be so fucking happy, and you know what, I am."

"Then what is it?"

"I liked taking care of her. I hated fucking up, and I'm not talking about that. I'm talking about the success of taking care of her. Helping her when the furniture moved, counting steps, cooking for her. Everything. I loved it."

"You're a man in love."

"Now though, she cooks for me all the time, and I'm having to count fucking steps or at least watch where I'm going. She's always moving stuff around the damn place, and I get it."

"Pussy, you talk to Sasha about this and she'll put you straight."

"I sound like a fucking pussy." He rubbed his eyes. "I don't even know what's wrong with me."

"For the first time in our lives we're not in any danger. Our clubs are stable. We're in one place. You're in love, and now it's time to show that woman how much you fucking love her. I've seen the way she looks at you, and there's no way she'd ever want you to be anywhere else."

"You should have been a fucking therapist, boss."

"Ha, you think so?"

"I know so. You always know what you're talking about." Pussy slapped him on the back.

Devil watched him enter the club and sighed.

In recent years he'd become a therapist to his boys. His cell phone rang, and he picked it up.

"You got good news for me?"

"I always have good news. Everything has been arranged."

Devil pulled out a notebook as Russ gave him the details of the plane, arrival, and what he'd need. "Thanks, man, this means a lot."

"Yeah, don't get used to it."

"We'll see."

He hung up the phone. So now all he needed was to make sure his woman was ready and they were good to go.

Ripper and Judi had already said they'd take the kids.

Bringing up Lash's name on his phone, he pressed "call."

"What do I owe the pleasure? I thought you kissed Tiny's ass whenever you called." Lash was really getting into his stride being the Prez of The Skulls. It wasn't going to his head like Devil had once thought it would.

"Just checking in to make sure you're good to have Simon with you."

Lash chuckled. "Yep, you can bring him over if you want. We're good. Anthony doesn't get why he has to have a buddy, but Angel's talking to him."

"No sleepovers with Tabby," Devil said.

"Dude, I'll be surprised if Tabby has any time for him. She's dealing with school and spending a lot of time with Darcy right now. They'll be good."

Now he was much happier. He didn't mind Simon and Tabitha hanging out so long as there were a lot of people around. He knew what it was like to be young and in lust.

He wasn't being a fucking Grandpa just yet.

****

"You need a new wardrobe," Natalie said.

Lexie glanced down at her large sweatpants and shirt. They were comfortable. She'd gotten used to throwing them on as trouble seemed to come calling every single moment.

"I'm good."

"You're going away for a few days, so you have to wear something nice. It's, like, a code," Natalie said, grabbing a dress from off the rack where she was standing.

Lexie sighed and watched as Natalie held it up and looked at her.

"Try this on."

"I'm not a child, okay. I don't need to keep trying clothes on."

"Appease me. Come on. It's nearly closing time. The shop is empty, and we've already packaged all the orders that need to go. You know you want to." She gave the dress a little shake as if to tease her.

Lexie sighed. "Fine. Fine."

Leaving the safety of the counter, she walked over to Natalie and took the dress from her. She walked toward the dressing rooms and listened as the other woman kept gathering clothes for her to try on.

"I think it's safe to say that Devil when he gets you alone is going to want to rip all of your clothes off. That sounds so sexy, but you know it's going to happen."

Yeah, that was what she was afraid of.

Keeping her back to the mirror, Lexie removed the clothes and then pulled the dress on. It was one of the few items that didn't require a zipper, and she put the dress in place, running her hands down the fabric.

It fit really snugly.

Turning left then right, she looked in the mirror and sighed. This was a mistake.

"You got it on?" Natalie asked, sounding really close.

"Ye—"

Before she even finished Natalie had the curtain open. "You look amazing. I knew you would."

Natalie grabbed her hand, pulling her out of the stall.

"You know I can walk."

"I know, but you're also being little miss negative right now, so I am going to take charge of this moment."

Natalie stood behind her, forcing her to look in the mirror. "Look at how beautiful you are." Natalie had her hands on her hips, giving her no choice but to look at the mirror. The dress was in fact beautiful and perfect. She loved it instantly.

Lexie ran her hands down the fabric. This was one of the reasons she loved working here. She got to see women trying on their clothes and seeing the wonder as they fit perfectly to their bodies.

Natalie was one heck of a designer. She had that knack for knowing what a woman wanted.

"I love it," she said.

"It's time to throw away all those sweatpants, Lexie. I hope Devil can get through to you." Natalie gave her a hug, and for the next hour she was forced to change into multiple different outfits, from tight-fitting jeans to a bikini, which there was no chance of her wearing.

As she came out in the bikini, she hadn't heard anyone enter, but Devil stood there, watching.

Natalie had her hands clasped together. "Doesn't she look gorgeous?"

"Perfect," Devil said.

She couldn't cover herself up, not in front of him.

He'd know, and then they'd be alone together.

So instead of putting her hand in front of her body, she placed it on her hip. "You like it? Because I don't think this suits me for Vegas."

"We're not going to Vegas. Everything is in place for one of the Billionaires' islands. Just you and me, babe. An ocean, a beach, the perfect setting."

"Oh."

"Yep, so I think a bikini will be needed. I like that one, a lot. Do you want to give a little turn?" He stood with his arms folded, looking every part the deadly biker. Taking a deep breath, she gave a little twirl, walking slowly.

Once she faced him again, she saw that spark in his eyes that let her know he was thinking about a lot of dirty things.

"I'll leave you two alone." Natalie, the traitor, walked away.

"I better go and change."

She stood in the dressing room, but Devil didn't give her a chance to close the door. He placed a hand on her naked hip, and her body lit up at his touch. Staring up at him, she waited.

"I know something is up with you. I'm not even going to pretend that I don't see it."

"It's nothing."

"There's something there, and I don't know what happened for you to think that I wouldn't notice, but I do. When it comes to you, I notice everything. Our time together, it'll give us a chance to straighten these things out between us. I want you to pack all the things Natalie tells you to and don't argue, okay."

"Where are you going?"

"I'm driving Simon down to Fort Wills. He's already packed and ready. I'll stay there overnight and come back tomorrow. We leave in two days."

"Why don't we drop Simon off together then? Take all the kids?"

"I need you to get everything ready for them all to go to Judi's." He cupped her cheek. "I'm not going to back out of this, babe. For four days, you will be mine. No interruptions, and then we'll see what that problem is." He tilted her head back and dropped a kiss to her lips.

He moved so that he was near her ear. "And for four days I'm going to fuck you. I want to hear you scream and to beg for more."

She was already so hot, but at his words, the promise in them, she couldn't wait for their time alone.

Chapter Three

"You'll behave," Devil said.

"Dad, I got it, okay? I'll be a good boy. I'll eat all my vegetables and talk about school and stuff. I'll be the perfect boy." Simon rolled his eyes. "I know how to behave with friends."

Devil stared at his son. "I mean it."

"Dad, you really need to think more about Mom right now. She seems weird."

"I know. What do you think it is?"

"I don't know? She's old."

"Excuse me." Devil tensed up, glaring at his son.

"I don't mean it like that. I heard some of the guys talking at school, and they were talking about MILFs and stuff. Mom's a MILF, but I don't know what a MILF is. I don't always get the lingo."

"Mom I'd like to fuck," Devil said.

The look on Simon's face was fucking priceless. "Ugh, that shit's disgusting. Dad, I'm going to get suspended when I get home."

"And why would that be?"

"Because I've got some asses to kick. They called my mom a MILF, and I didn't knock their fucking faces."

"We'll deal with it."

Lash came out of the house with Anthony beside him.

"You know me and Anthony just put up with each other, right? He digs Daisy, and seein' as I'm seeing Tabby, that's why he keeps me around," Simon said.

"I don't give a fuck, bud. You're staying with Anthony, and if you want me off your case when you get suspended, you'll stay here."

"But Miles—"

"Lives with Tabitha."

"Dad, we're not going to do anything."

"Simon, son, don't treat me like a fucking idiot. I remember what it was like to be a kid your age."

"That was so long ago for you."

Devil smirked. "Insult me all you want. It's true, and I know what you're going through."

"I heard Mom muttering to herself that she's old and you don't want her anymore." Simon shrugged. "That's all I know. Later, Dad."

Devil watched his son walk up the steps. Anthony was glaring at him, and he smirked. They did get along to a point. Simon was a tough cookie. Lash came down the steps.

"You staying over?"

"I'm heading over to Tiny and Eva's. Figured one Chaos Bleeds in your household was enough," Devil said.

Lash looked over his shoulder and laughed as Anthony's hand was counting stuff off. "He's giving him the ground rules. I told him to handle Simon. It's good to keep him active."

"He still playing with knives?"

Lash sighed. "Yes, and he likes cutting things. Not himself or animals, but he's started helping Angel in the kitchen, which has given him something to do."

"You think all the bad shit has gone to his head?"

"I think Anthony is just a little different is all. I was similar at his age. It'll pass."

Lash had a coldness inside him. He was a mean motherfucker who could snap a man's neck with his own two hands.

"So, I got a call from Russ," Lash said.

Devil chuckled. "Yeah?"

"Yeah, he asked if I wanted any special favors,

seeing as you'd already called them in."

"We gave them back their fucking money, Lash. I don't need them to pay for shit."

"I'm pleased you did," Lash said.

"Why?"

"Because ... Darcy needs help, and with the Billionaires having all that extra cash, I called in a favor as well," Lash said. "For Blaine, Emily, and Darcy."

"Shit, is it that bad?"

"It is, but I think with the right team, she'll be okay."

Devil nodded. "She's just a kid."

"I know, and now she's having to grow up real fucking fast," Lash said. "I can't even imagine what she's going through right now."

"Lash, dinner's ready," Angel said, coming to the door.

"I'll be right there." Lash looked back at him. "You sure you don't want some food?"

"Nope. Tiny and Eva are already expecting me."

"Good look. We'll take good care of your boy." Lash slapped him on the back.

Climbing into the car, Devil pulled away from Lash's home. He knew Simon would be taken care of. There was no point in putting him with Judi and Ripper. Simon would just push his boundaries and then he'd get a call to come and help.

Judi and Simon took their sibling problems way too seriously. Simon liked being a pain in the ass.

Lash would keep him in line, of that Devil had no doubt.

Pulling up outside of Tiny and Eva's place, he stared up at the house. Simon's words echoed around in his head, and it made him curious.

Lexie hadn't been the same since the picnic, and

he'd been a little worried that it had to do with the luxury that the Billionaires had to offer. He offered her a good life but nothing to that scale. He was so far out of his fucking league when it came to the Billionaires' wealth. Now though, it seemed Lexie was having an altogether different problem.

It made him smile.

If Lexie truly believed that she was too old for him and that he didn't want her, she was very much mistaken.

He had to keep himself in check half the time when he was around her. There were times he was annoyed that they had so many kids because it meant they didn't have as much time together. Of course, he loved his kids. They were part of him and Lexie, but he was a selfish bastard. He wanted his woman all to himself, and he wasn't used to having to share.

"You okay?" Tiny asked, knocking on the window.

"Just trying to have a few moments of peace but clearly I can't have that."

Tiny laughed. "Eva made dinner, and we're all waiting."

"Excellent." He was going to show Lexie just how much he fucking wanted her. She wasn't going to be able to walk by the time he was done with her.

****

Lexie's bags were all packed and ready to go. She'd even put all of Devil's stuff in a suitcase, and he was ready as well. All of their kids' things were ready, and she was putting them in the car. Devil had told her to drop them off with Ripper and Judi before meeting him at the clubhouse.

With the kids all in place, she quickly checked the house one last time before climbing into the driver's seat.

Pulling out of the driveway, she made her way toward Ripper and Judi's, which wasn't far, but she had no interest in trying to carry all of them and their bags and cases.

Ripper was mowing his lawn as she pulled up, and Judi sat with a book as their kids played around her.

They moved toward the car, helping her take the children out. Their excited screams filled the air as she handed over the information sheet she'd prepared last night, along with their clothes and some money.

"You do know we can take care of them. You don't have to pay us for this."

Lexie nodded. "I know. I also know that … it helps."

"They're going to be well taken care of," Ripper said.

"I know. I know."

She crouched down, and one by one her babies came toward her, throwing their arms around her neck, hugging her close. This was her family.

Getting to her feet, Judi held Ameila, the youngest of them all, also, their last child as Devil had gotten fixed so that he couldn't have any more children.

She knew herself that she wouldn't be able to carry many more after Ameila. Pregnancy exhausted her.

"Please, call if something happens or if you need some advice or something."

"We'll take good care of them, Lex," Ripper said.

"Right."

Judi held her tightly. "Go and have some good times. You deserve it."

Lexie nodded and climbed back into the car.

Driving toward the clubhouse took a little longer. She kept the windows down even though there was a bit of a chill in the air. Summer was leaving, and soon it would be fall and winter. Halloween, Thanksgiving, and Christmas were right around the corner and with it came a lot of work. Costumes, food, preparations for everything.

She drove up into the carpark of the clubhouse. Devil was already there, arms folded, talking with Vincent.

Devil moved to the driver's door, and she moved across to the passenger seat.

"Is everything okay?"

"Yep, just catching up with Vincent as he dropped by. You ready?"

"Yeah, I guess. I don't mind if you've got other plans that have come up. We can let Simon have his sleepover and we'll be fine."

"Babe, I'm not going to pass up the chance to be alone with you. Not anymore."

"Great."

She ran her hands down her legs. Her palms were a little sweaty.

Devil took one in his and pressed a kiss to her knuckles. When she made to pull away, he locked their fingers together as he pulled out of the clubhouse.

"This seems kind of crazy, doesn't it? Leaving them after everything."

"They all know what to do, and if they really need me, they'll call. I'm not going to come running if one of them falls over and has grazed knees."

They had been away so many times alone before. Sometimes they had a couple of kids with them. This was new though. At least to her it was new.

Being away with him after feeling like this.

She loved him so much, but she couldn't seem to go back.

"Is Simon behaving?" she asked.

"Best behavior. He knows what's good for him. When he goes back to school, he'll … erm, might cause a few problems."

"Why?" Lexie asked.

"Let's just say he's got a rep to protect and a mom to take care of."

"Wait, what do I have to do with all this?"

Devil was laughing. "You're a MILF."

"What?" Lexie asked. She hadn't caught that right.

"With all the talk in the club, you'd think our boy would understand what it means. He didn't realize that his friends were calling you that."

"Wow," she said. "That seems so … weird. MILF."

"Please tell me you know what it means."

"I know what it means." She chuckled. "Poor Simon."

"They're not wrong though."

"Devil."

"I'm being serious here. If there was a woman like you going to the school, I'd totally befriend Simon. Also, I'd start trying to figure out a way to get you into bed. You are a woman I want to fuck and always want to."

Her cheeks heated. "They're kids."

"Kids with dicks still. I think the problem with the world right now, they underestimate these kids. They want to treat them as delicate creatures when, believe me, they're far from it."

She rested her head against his shoulder. She had missed this so much. Missed him and it felt good to be talking to him again.

"Simon won't be bringing any friends around

either."

She burst out laughing. "You're jealous?"

"Nope, protecting what is mine, and I'm not getting any younger. I can't have you drooling over all the young stallions that come through our home."

"There's no competition," she said. "There never was."

Devil glanced over at her. "Then I hope you realize the same thing."

"What?"

"There's no one else for me. You're perfect no matter what."

She thought about her body in the mirror, and she really hoped he was right. Doubt plagued her thoughts. She didn't pull away from him though. Resting her head on his arm, she tried her best to ignore that voice that kept telling her she wasn't good enough.

For once she wanted to ignore it all.

Chapter Four

Russ wasn't kidding when he said he wouldn't spare any expense. The island was a dream. They had to be flown in via private helicopter, not that it was a problem. The views were incredible.

Devil watched as Lexie basked in all the glory, and it truly was an amazing sight to behold. There were a couple of men and women waiting for them who gave them a note, along with instructions. The house was huge, of course it was. Fully furnished, complete with a pool, game room, and everything a billionaire could want and everyone else dreamed of.

"Wow," she said. "This is just ... like something out of a magazine."

"Yeah, well, it looks like I can get this place whenever I want." He dropped their bags on the floor and pulled her against him. "Now that we're all alone and no one can interrupt us."

"I better phone home and make sure everything is okay."

She made to pull out of his arms, but he wasn't buying that.

"They're fine. You need to stop worrying about everything." He ran his hands up and down her back, and she sighed.

"Fine. Fine. You're right."

"Of course I'm right. I'm right about everything."

She smiled. "Some things never change with you."

"You'll see that a lot doesn't change with me, babe. Nothing." He watched the smile fall from her face. "But, *you're* changing. Something is up, and I want to know what it is."

"It's nothing."

"Lex, baby, I'm not going to let you hide from me. Now, I want you to go to the bathroom, relax. Take a long bath. I'm going to put us something to eat in the oven."

"You're going to cook?"

"I can handle a few things. Then I'm going to come and join you."

"What about the kids?"

"I'm their dad. I'll phone them."

She nibbled her lip.

"This is for you and me and I'm not taking no for an answer, so you may as well do as you're asked."

She rolled her eyes. "Fine."

He slapped her on the ass as she walked away, and she let out a little yelp.

"There'll be more where that comes from."

"You're crazy."

"And you love it."

She winked at him, and he watched her go. Damn, that was a fine ass. He loved watching her no matter what.

Pulling out his cell phone, he headed into the kitchen.

"You made it there safely?" Angel asked.

"You've got that right. Now, you promised me you'd help me out here."

"You do know over the phone there's only so much I can do."

"And I know you can work magic. I have faith in you, Angel. Let's make this happen."

With the phone on speaker he listened as Angel instructed him on how to make one of Lexie's favorite dishes, spicy baked chicken with potatoes and tomatoes. Russ had come through for him on all counts from the house to the food, to everything. He owed him big time, which he didn't mind. Lexie was worth it.

"Bake all that in the oven for about an hour and you'll be good to serve up and eat."

"Right." He slid the dish into the oven. "Done. Pudding? Shit, what do I do for pudding?"

"Check your fridge. Do you have strawberries, chocolate syrup, and cream?"

"Yeah."

"You've got a sexy pudding, and you don't need to stress. Lexie will love all that you've done for her."

"Thanks, Angel. I really appreciate it."

"No problem. I can't wait to see what we come up with for Valentine's Day."

"How's my son?" he asked.

"Simon's good. He's a bit moody because Anthony won't go over to Tiny and Eva's, but that's understandable. Tabby's grounded."

"She is?"

"Yep, she got in a fight at school. Beat the shit out of a boy. She won't tell the school why, so they suspended her."

"Sounds shifty to me."

"It does, but they don't want her going around beating up everyone. I've got to go. Take care, Devil."

He hung up the phone and quickly placed a call to Ripper. All the kids were fine, just as he expected.

Now, he had a woman to go and deal with.

It didn't take him long to find the bathroom. Standing in the doorway, he watched her lie back, her nipples appearing above the water, most of her covered in a layer of bubbles. Lexie looked sexy as fuck.

Removing his leather cut, he began to strip down. He couldn't remember the last time they were alone together.

They always had to be quiet so they didn't wake

the kids. Lexie wasn't usually a quiet woman, and now he wanted to hear his name screamed from her lips, echoing around the room.

Entering the bathroom, his cock stood out rock-hard and ready for her.

She opened her eyes and smiled up at him. "I can tell what's on your mind."

"Budge forward then."

"This is my bath," she said.

"And now I need to clean you up."

"Something smells good," she said.

"It'll smell better in fifty minutes." Climbing into the water, he wrapped his arms around her, and he noticed she placed her hand between his and her stomach.

For the past couple of weeks, he'd noticed these little changes in Lexie. She wouldn't change in the bedroom if he was there and the light was on. She'd take her clothes into the bathroom, even her pajamas. Whenever he got to touch her, the light would be turned off, or she'd complain of a headache.

He didn't like fucking in the dark. Never had.

When he took Lexie, he liked to see his cock sliding inside her naked pussy lips, fucking her, taking her again and again. It was one of the reasons she ended up pregnant so often. He just couldn't get enough of her.

Taking hold of her wrist, he locked them both together and held her hands above her head.

"What the hell are you doing?" she asked.

"I could say the same to you. Why are you constantly trying to avoid my touch? Do I not do it for you anymore, baby?"

"You don't know what you're talking about."

"Oh, believe me, I do. More than you even know."

****

With her hands locked above her head, there was no way of escaping. Lexie should have known that Devil would see and know something was up. He held her wrists together in one of his and then ran his other hand down her body. He started at her shoulder then down to cup her tit.

He circled the hardened bud with the tip of a finger.

"There's my girl. Sexy, hot, and wanting me. Now I don't know what has gotten into you of late. You won't change in front of me, nor will you let me fuck you with the light on. You think I don't notice these things, but I do. Believe me, I fucking do, and it's tearing me apart to see you like this." He traced a finger across the valley between her tits, circling her other nipple.

She was so sensitive that an answering wave of pleasure rushed over her. Her clit started to pulse, and she wanted him so much.

Devil always knew what to do to make her body come alive and to make her want him. Not that it was hard to do, she always wanted him. He stopped teasing her nipples to cup her tits. Suddenly he stopped and held both of her hands and wrapped them around his neck so that she was holding onto him.

"You do not let go. If you do and try and stop me, I won't let you come for the entire night, do you understand?"

She whimpered. "Devil."

"Yes or no?"

"Yes."

"Good. I'm going to play with you, and I don't want you arguing with me, understand? I know what you need, and I'm going to be the one to give it to you just like I am always going to give it to you."

He kissed her neck, sucking on her pulse. Closing her eyes, she let herself go.

"Now," he said, putting his hands on her hips. "Let's start at the beginning. Ah, yes, Lexie, you're my wife. The mother of all of my children. The very reason I fucking breathe at times. Why are you hiding yourself from me?"

"I don't mean to."

He pinched her nipples, making her cry out. "Don't lie to me."

She loved the pleasure and pain. It had been so long since they could have this. She didn't want it to stop.

"I'm not young anymore. I'm not a stripper anymore."

"Baby, you've not been a stripper in a long time. You're all mine. I don't share what's mine."

"You're … what if you don't want me?" She tilted her head back, looking at him. If he wanted the truth, she'd give it to him. "I'm not a fool, Devil. I know some men in clubs take on extra women. Screw the sweet-butts and never commit to their wives." She groaned. "Damn, I didn't want to tell you this."

She released his neck and stood up. She got out of the tub, dripping wet, and was about to grab a towel when Devil picked her up around the waist and carried her through to the bedroom. He held her as if she weighed nothing.

"Let me go, Devil."

"Not happening, babe." He dropped her to the bed but didn't let her go alone. He followed her right down, capturing her hands in his.

"You can't do this," she said.

"Actually, I kind of am, and you're not going to argue."

He straddled her waist, and she stared up at him, wriggling.

"You know, you look so fucking sexy. Those tits bouncing. I really do love your tits, Lexie."

"Can't we talk about this?"

"I want to talk about this. Don't get me wrong, I think your reasoning is so fucking stupid, but I'm happy to talk about this. You think I've got a problem with you getting older? With you getting fuller?"

"I'm not the same woman you met."

"No, and I'm not the same man that busted down your apartment door, but I'm not going to run and hide. I expected more of you, Lex."

She gritted her teeth, staring up at him.

"We're in this together. You and me. A team, a partnership. It's us, and it will always be us against those fucking kids. You're the one person in the world that I cannot live without. I'm fucking insulted that you'd even think so low as me to even take a woman on the side. Even now, my dick is hard for you, and only you. Other women don't even register on my radar. I don't even know what to say to this shit now. When have I ever given you a reason to fucking doubt me?"

Tears filled her eyes as she saw the pain that Devil would only ever let her see. She had hurt him. Her doubt had cut him deep.

"Devil?"

"Before I met you, I didn't give a fuck about anyone. Kayla didn't mean anything. When I found out I had a kid, I couldn't give a fuck. He was mine, and I was going to do right by him. No matter what anyone said. Then I saw you at that club, and I wanted you. I've never wanted or craved a woman like I do you. These feelings, they don't go away, Lex. They only get stronger. I think about you all the time. If you must know, my feelings for you are getting stronger every single day that we're together. That's how I feel. The way you look, the shape of your body, to me you are and will always be perfect." He shook his head. "I'm going to check on dinner."

He climbed off her, leaving her feel open and raw.

She had hurt him, and now she felt like the worst person in the world. She had to fix this.

Chapter Five

The chicken was done, but right now, Devil was so fucking pissed off. This hadn't been his plan for a romantic getaway. This was supposed to be his and Lexie's time with each other. How could she even think he'd want someone else? He'd never in all the years together given her any reason to doubt him.

Fuck, he'd even surprised himself.

Lexie had changed him. No matter how cliché it sounded, she had made him a better fucking man. He strived to be the kind of man she deserved.

Checking dinner, he saw it was cooked, and pulled it out. He was completely naked, but right then, he didn't care. If Russ had cameras in this place, he'd kill him, simple as that. He'd gladly shed some blood right about now.

He placed the chicken on the counter just as Lexie came in. She wore a robe, and he wasn't happy. "I made you your favorite."

"How did you know how to cook it?"

"I have my means." He gripped the edge of the counter. Silence stretched between them, and he hated that. They never were like this with each other. They could always share their secrets, their pains, their problems.

"I'm sorry," she said.

"When did you start feeling this way?" he asked.

"After the picnic. It's stupid."

"No, it's not stupid."

She looked around her. "This is really not our place."

"I know, but I wanted the best for you. I love you, Lexie. I always have." He stared at the food, his stomach rumbling.

"I didn't mean to say that stuff. I really shouldn't have said anything."

"No, I want you to be honest with me. It's the only way I can know what is going on with you."

He grabbed them some plates and a serving spoon and started to portion their food. Placing one in front of Lexie, he took a seat on the chair.

"You're not going to put any clothes on?"

"I'm on vacation with my wife. I'm not planning on wearing any clothes. You really didn't need to pack me anything."

She chuckled. "It's been a long time since we've been able to sit naked."

"*I* am sitting naked. You're not."

He saw her cheeks heat and then watched as she unbelted the robe and let it fall down all around her. Some of the robe stayed on the seat, protecting her butt.

"Perfect," he said.

"I didn't want to hurt you."

"I know."

"I just … it's hard, you know. I guess you don't."

"You think I don't get it. We've got an age difference here, Lex. I came into your life an old man. That hasn't changed. I'm getting older, and you're beautiful. Any man would be so fucking happy to have you at their side. I know what I've got, and I've no intention of ever screwing that shit up. You can believe me or not, but I told you, I'm in this for life. My dick has your name on it. Always. Now, try your food."

He watched as Lexie took a bite. Her eyes went wide. "Wow, that's actually really good."

"Don't sound so surprised. I had Angel talk me through it. I can follow instructions."

He took a bite and was rather impressed. The meal was perfect. The seduction though needed a lot of work.

They finished their meal in silence, but it wasn't uncomfortable. Over the years they'd shared many meals in silence. Once they were finished, he made Lexie sit down while he did the dishes, catching her eyeing his ass.

Afterward, he took her hand and led her through to the sitting room. He moved the coffee table out of the way and took a seat. When Lexie made to sit with him, he shook his head. "I want you to show me where you think there's a problem."

"Devil?"

He stood up. "I have wrinkles, and my ass is a bit saggy now. I see myself aging. What don't you like on me?"

"I love every single part of you, and you know it."

Stepping up to her, he took her hands. "Then why can't you accept that I love every single part of you?" He kissed her knuckles on each hand. Sinking to his knees before her, he pressed a kiss to her rounded stomach. "Why can't you accept that I love you the way you are? That you turn me on being this way."

He grabbed her ass before pressing his face against her pussy. Breathing her in, he only scented his woman. The love of his life.

Lexie was the only person in the world to him that he'd ever be like this with.

"I hate myself right about now," she said, her fingers stroking through his hair.

"Don't hate yourself." He kissed her stomach, moving her back so that she sat on the chair. "Tell me what you hate about yourself? What you think I don't like?"

"I'm older."

"We've been together a long time. If I was only interested in your age, I'd have been looking for a newer model years ago."

"Devil," she said.

"I'm being honest. It's not your age or your looks, or your tits and ass that I like. I love *you*, Lexie, the entire package, and if I have to spend this time with you proving it to you, then I will. I will do anything for you."

She cupped his cheek. "I believe you. I can't believe I would even think for a second that you'd cheat. I know you wouldn't. I trust you. I love you so much."

"Good. I love you too. For the rest of this vacation you're going to prove it to me by not wearing a single thing."

"I can't do that."

"Yeah, you can. It's just you and me. I want to see my wife naked. I want to watch her run down the beach with nothing between us. Come on, we've got nothing to lose. No kids to barge in. What do you say?"

****

Staring into his eyes, Lexie knew he wouldn't lie to her. The doubts she had were all her fault. Not once had he given her reason to believe that he was wrong.

"Yes," she said. "I want to have this with you." She sat up, cupping his cheek. Pressing her lips against his, she moaned as he gripped the back of her head, kissing her harder, their teeth clashing with their need for each other.

Devil broke the kiss, pressing her back against the sofa. With his gaze still on her, he placed his hands on her knees. He spread her legs open then ran his hands up her thighs, underneath her, cupping her ass before pulling her forward so that she was near the edge of the sofa.

He still hadn't looked at her body yet, his eyes on

her face. The way he kept watching her though, it was like he wanted to eat her.

"My cock is so hard right now. I'm going to eat your pussy, and I want you to scream my name as I do."

"Yes."

"I want you to spread yourself open for me. Show me your cunt, Lexie."

She reached down between them and, using her fingers, opened the lips of her pussy so he saw her.

His gaze moved down her body, going from her tits until he came to her pussy. He moaned. "Now that is a pretty little cunt right there, and it's all mine."

She gasped as he slid a finger down her slit, pushing inside her. He added a second finger, rocking back and forth. He pulled his finger out of her pussy, sliding it up to stroke her clit.

"Watch me, Lex. Watch me play with you."

Staring between her spread legs, she saw his hand moving through her slit, teasing her clit then down to enter her, before drawing back to continue to play.

The pleasure was immense, but it wasn't enough to make her come, just enough to make her desperate and begging for more.

He drew his fingers back and sucked them into his mouth. "You taste so good."

She cried out as his mouth latched onto her clit, sucking and nibbling at the bud. He stroked back and forth but not staying long before moving down, plunging inside her, fucking her.

She arched up, needing more and more of his touch, but he wouldn't give it to her exactly how she liked. He was torturing her, making her beg for more.

"You're all mine, Lexie. All fucking mine and everything you do is for me and me alone. You have no idea just how fucking much I want you, crave you, need you. There's nothing I wouldn't do for you because I love you so fucking much."

His fingers moved between her thighs, and she felt him fucking her to the knuckle. He was back with two and three fingers, stretching her.

"Let me hear you scream, Lexie. We don't have to hold anything back. I want to hear you. Don't stop."

She didn't hold back her moans as he continued to lick and suck at her pussy. She watched his tongue dance across her clit and enjoyed the feel of his fingers. They were not as big as his cock, but they made her ache in all the right ways.

Her orgasm started to build, and as she was about to get to that peak, he suddenly stopped, pressing a kiss to her clit.

"Devil, why did you stop?" she asked.

Her entire body was shaken.

He sat back, wiping his face. "I can never get over how good you taste."

"Devil?"

"Oh, yeah, you let go of my neck in the bath."

"Wait? What? I … we're not done here."

He shrugged. "You're right, we're not. I'll be in the pool when you're ready."

She watched him get to his feet and walk away.

Her mouth was open, and she was shocked that he'd actually leave her like this. How could he leave her … so desperate?

You doubted him.

Gritting her teeth, she was tempted to bring herself off, but she knew she wouldn't do as good a job of it as Devil. Grabbing the nearest pillow, she released a scream. Devil would make her pay for thinking that she wasn't good enough.

She got to her feet and made her way toward the

kitchen, which led out the back.

Devil was on his back in the pool. His cock was hard, she saw all the way from the kitchen. This wasn't about the two of them fighting. She had no interest in that.

You've got to get your shit together.

Going out there, he won.

Staying inside, she lost.

She wanted him. All of her problems were her own doing. Clenching her hands into fists, she decided to ignore them. Stepping out into the garden, she folded her arms and watched Devil. He truly was a magnificent man. Strong, fearless, determined; the best kind of person she'd ever known. He looked death in the face and laughed while he did. Throughout all of their troubles with the club, she knew he'd never let anything happen to her or their family.

Chaos Bleeds was their family as well.

"Have you decided to join me?" he asked.

"I'm not sure. I'm still annoyed at myself. I can't believe I accused you of cheating. I mean, what is wrong with me? I'm so stupid."

"Those feelings will pass when I'm inside you."

"Your ego knows no bounds."

"It's not about the ego, babe. I know what to do with myself, and I don't need to have an ego when I make you come." He stood up in the water. "I don't want you to ever feel like I don't want you. Bottling that shit up won't do between us. You can hide it from the others, by all means. You and me, we're together forever."

She smiled. Stepping into the pool, she walked up toward him. "Together forever."

"That's right. I made you a vow and a promise. I will keep them, Lex. For better or for worse. I will love you for the rest of our lives."

Chapter Six

Lexie wrapped her arms around his neck. Devil gripped her hips, holding her as she wrapped her legs around him. He padded over to the steps, sitting down, and she straddled his waist.

Cupping the back of her head, he brought her down to kiss.

"Please don't torture me all night. I'll do whatever you want."

"I want to go walking down the beach completely naked. Will you do that with me?" he asked.

"What is it with you and walking naked everywhere?"

"We're on a private island. Chances are, we won't get to do this again. Might as well cross some things off our bucket list."

"Running around naked is on our bucket list?"

"Running around naked with you is on my bucket list." He ran his hand up her back before sliding back down to cup her ass.

"Is this bucket list long?"

"It's reasonable."

"I want you inside me," she said.

He chuckled. "Then put me inside you."

Lifting her up, he watched and counted as she grabbed his cock, placing it at her entrance. Slowly, he brought her down over his cock, filling her.

"You're so fucking beautiful," he said. "I don't even know why you're doubting my feelings for you. There's no one else in the world I could ever want."

Inch by inch, he filled her to the hilt. She arched her back, gasped, and ground her pussy on his dick. He felt every twinge and pulse of her cunt around his dick.

Lifting her up, he began to rock her on his dick,

watching her take him.

Up and down, he slammed inside her, unable to look away.

"This bucket list?" she asked.

"I want to run on the beach naked with you."

She let out a laugh followed by a moan as he bounced her on his cock.

"We've done a lot of what I want to do."

"Such as?"

"Fuck while we're on a picnic. Take your ass. Get you knocked up. Make you beg me. Spank your ass for being a naughty girl."

He gripped her butt so hard that he knew he'd leave marks. She had such a fucking hot ass. He was going to fuck it, hear her scream for more as he did.

"I can't think when you do that."

"Good, I don't want you to think about anything but me."

He spread the cheeks of her ass open, sliding a hand between them, feeling her puckered asshole. "You want me to fuck your ass."

The last time he'd been inside her, Simon had walked in, and of course, he'd ended up throwing shit at his son to get out. Lexie had told him until he either put a lock on the door or the kids moved out, anal was for special occasions.

Yeah, having his son see his naked ass was never going to be something he went for. That shit even scarred him.

"Yes."

"Oh, baby, we're going to have so much fun."

Her hands went to his shoulders, and she began to work her pussy up and down his length. He watched her take him, his dick coated in her cream.

"I want to come, Devil."

"Do you want to come all over my cock?"

"Yes."

Releasing her ass, he stroked through her clit, seeing her eyes dilate, and she rocked on him a little faster, taking him a little harder. It was so fucking sexy, watching her come apart like that.

He couldn't get enough of her.

She was so hot, so ready, all his.

Devil couldn't believe she had ever doubted his love for her, or even his need. He was a fucking horn dog when it came to this woman.

There was nothing he wouldn't do for her.

She was the perfect woman as far as he was concerned.

He felt the first fluttering inside her pussy as she got closer to orgasm. Stroking her tight cunt, he waited, watching her, completely hypnotized as she gave herself to him. Lexie never held anything back. She gave all of herself, an equal of passion and need.

"Please, Devil."

"Come for me, baby. I'll give you this orgasm. Show my dick some loving."

She held onto him and then screamed his name as she came hard. Her cunt tightened around him like a vise, not giving up.

He played with her until she could no longer stand his touch. Grabbing her hips, he started to fuck her. Drawing her up and down his length, he took what belonged to him, and Lexie was his in every single way that counted. So beautiful and perfect.

There were no words that could even begin to describe what she meant to him.

Over and over, he pounded away inside her pussy, hungry for her. Horny, desperate, ready.

Plunging into her one final time, he spilled his

cum into her waiting pussy. She wrapped her arms around his neck, and he felt that change within her.

Before they had arrived at the island, the connection between them had been severed. Lexie had been different. Now, she was back. All his, and in his arms. He was never going to let her go again, nor was he going to give her the chance of thinking he would never love her.

No matter their kids, he would make sure that she knew he wanted her.

When they got home, the kids were going to have to learn some boundaries because there was no way he was waiting this long to hear his wife come or to make love to her.

"I love you, Devil, always."

He held her tightly, not wanting to let go. Pushing some of her hair off her face, he smiled up at her. "Always. You own me, woman. I've never said that to another living soul."

****

"We really shouldn't do this," Lexie said.

She watched as Devil stretched out his muscles. He clearly didn't have a care in the world, which was incredibly hot. His arms were out, and he was butt-ass naked, all of his ink on full display. This was what she missed so much.

Not his naked body. She saw that every single day.

No, it was how open he was with her. Back at home, he always had to be in charge as either leader of Chaos Bleeds or as the father to her children. When they were alone together, he changed before her eyes, and she got to see the real him that he kept hidden. If only people knew he had a playful side. Women would flock to him, which was another reason she adored him.

He allowed only her to see this side.

"No one is around, and no one is here to stop us. We're not breaking any rules here. We can make them as we go along." He held his hands out. "Come on, baby. Run with me."

She rolled her eyes. "I'll wobble."

"And I'll love every single inch of you."

"Fine."

She grabbed the belt of her robe, but he caught her to him.

"Let me do the honors."

"You're always trying to find new ways of getting me out of clothes."

"You love it."

She really did.

He opened the robe and slid it off her shoulders where it fell to the ground. She took a deep breath. There was no hiding now. He could see every single inch of her and then some more.

Lexie placed her arms on his shoulders as his hands once again went to her hips. Everything faded away, and all her focus was on this man, the love of her life.

"Are you ready?"

"I still think this is crazy."

"But fun crazy." With that, he took her hand, and she screamed as they ran across the edge of the beach. The ocean was so beautiful, and she couldn't stop laughing as they ran the length and then finally collapsed at the end.

She fell to the ground on her back, staring up at the sky.

"I will never forget what that feels like," he said.

He dropped down beside her, pulling her against him. She rested her head on his chest. "You won't."

"No, I loved every fucking second of that." He kissed her lips. He pulled her across him, and she sat up straddling his waist. "Tell me something you love about me," he said.

"Really? You're going to ask that?"

"You girls are always asking us guys. It's time I got a bit back."

She chuckled. "You want to know what I love about you?"

"Yes."

"You'll have to tell me what you love about me."

"Have you got the rest of your life to listen to that?" he asked.

"You say the sweetest things."

"Just keeping it real, baby."

"Fine, I love your ass."

"I do have a fine ass, babe. Just like you." He gripped her ass, and the pleasure rushed through her body.

"Your eyes, your nose, and I certainly love your mouth and your tongue."

He showed her his tongue, and she giggled. "It's all for you."

"I love your sense of humor. I love the fact that I'm the only one that gets to see it. That you're real with me."

"Always."

"I love you being Prez. It turns me on to see you taking charge. It's your club, and you know more than anyone how to look after it."

"Chaos Bleeds is in my blood. I'll do whatever I can to protect it."

"Your loyalty to The Skulls. Accepting Tiny stepping down. Making friends with him. Not holding a grudge."

"There's more important shit to life than holding shit locked in like that. I accepted Tiny's decision 'cause he knew it was his time to step down."

She touched his cheek. "And I love that you're a great father. Even when they all piss you off. You're always going to be there for them."

"They're my babies. They're part of you, Lex. That makes them good people in my book."

Her cheeks heated. "You always know when to say the right thing."

"It's part of my charm, which I see *didn't* make your list."

"I love the entire package, Devil. Your charm is still not up to Ned's standard."

"That old fucker wouldn't even know what to do with a woman like you."

"A woman like me?"

"Yeah, my woman. A woman who is confident."

She snorted. "You wouldn't have believed that when we arrived."

"We all have our moments."

"You do?" she asked.

"What?"

"Have you ever had a moment when you've been scared? When you've not known what to do?" she asked.

He stared at her for the longest time. "Yes." He spoke the word so quietly.

"When?"

"That day in the kitchen. Gonzalez was there, and he held you against the kitchen counter. I've never been so fucking afraid in all my life. Then the day when they opened fire on The Skulls' clubhouse. We had our babies there, and you were there. Everything happened so fast, even now I can't remember it all. I know that losing you will end me because I will spend the rest of my life hunting the fuckers that took you from me and when it was all over, I'll join you."

"No, Devil."

"Yes. You think I'll be able to live going home every day and not having you there? While you were in the hospital, I've thought about it. I can't handle that. I know that will break me. It's why I have everything in place that if anything happens to you, Ripper and Pussy get the kids."

"Ripper and Pussy? Why those two?"

"Because our kids are Chaos Bleeds. Otherwise I'd have them go to Tiny and Lash. They're my decisions based on the men I've seen them become."

"I can't … no, I don't like that, Devil. You have to be around to take care of our kids."

"I'm not going to argue with you on this."

Chapter Seven

Devil poured the sunscreen into his palms, rubbing them together before running them all over Lexie's back. She lay spread out, hands beneath her head, chin resting on her clasped hands.

"I don't like that."

"Lex?"

"No, I know you're all about joining me and stuff, but what if I don't leave from someone taking me out?"

His hands clenched into fists. Just the thought of anyone hurting his woman made him want to fucking kill. Protecting her was his main priority. It's why he'd stopped the illegal runs and turned toward more legal activities with regards to the deal they had with Granito and of course now siding with the right side of the Billionaire Bikers. He would never have done any of this if it wasn't for Lexie.

"I know you hate hearing about this, but you really don't have much choice. If you die, I'd have to keep on going, or will you want me to kill myself to join you?"

"Of course not."

"Then I mean it, Devil. If you kill yourself to be with me, wherever I go, I'll make your life a misery because I need to know that our babies will be protected. I hate this kind of talk when you have it, but seeing as you're the one that brought it up, I've got no choice but to do this."

He sighed. He should have just kept his mouth shut.

"Our kids have the right to grow up with a father."

"And a mother."

"Yes, and if one of us should go, then I expect either you or myself to be selfless and to be there for them. Imagine all of our kids with nowhere to turn. I don't want that. With one of us, at least they'll have a fighting chance."

She rolled over, and for a few seconds he was distracted by her tits. Lexie clicked her fingers. "I'm up here."

He stared at her, brow raised, waiting.

"I mean it, Devil." She took his hand. "I know you love me, and I know before coming here my own insecurities were in my head. Before we go home, I need to know that you'll consider our children."

"Woman, you make this really fucking hard."

"I know." She kissed his hand.

He knew if he didn't agree she'd be pissed.

The truth was he only saw her leaving him because some fucker had gotten to him, not for any other reason. They were getting older.

Some reasons could come in many different shapes and sizes. He didn't like it. He would hate to have anything happen to her, but that was the point. Anything could happen to her. He'd be fucking lost and heartbroken. She'd never forgive him, and that alone made him nod.

"I will."

"You promise, Devil? To always be here for our kids no matter what."

"I keep my promises, Lexie. I will do everything in my power to keep them safe and be here for them if … anything was to happen to you."

She cupped his face, smiling.

"Now, I'm going to fuck you." He flipped her over on the sun lounger, lifting her so that she was on her knees.

She released a little giggle. "You just can't get enough, can you?"

He found her entrance and slid inside.

Her pussy was tight, pulsing around him.

"When it comes to you, I can't seem to get enough of anything." He pulled out only to slam back in. Gripping her hips, he pounded his dick in deep, watching his cock slide in and out of her pussy, stretching her.

Just watching her take him aroused him. He was never going to get enough of her perfect body, dripping cunt, and sexy as fuck pussy.

Spreading her ass, he saw her puckered hole. Before they left he intended to take that for himself once again.

Lexie's cries rang out, and he relished those sounds. He hated fucking in silence. What was the fun in being quiet? He wanted to hear her moans, the desperate pleas for more. He never wanted it to end.

From that first moment he saw her, dancing around that pole, getting naked, his dick had become hers. Then, getting to know her, seeing the love of the woman she was, she'd claimed his heart. Piece by piece, she'd unraveled him until the only thing that remained was that he was owned by her.

No matter the promise she demanded, he'd give it to her.

Some men would consider him pussy-whipped, and that was more than fine with him. He was pussy-whipped. In fact, he was fucking addicted.

Driving inside her, he slid one hand down her back, wrapping her hair around his fist, and the other he slid between her thighs, stroking her clit.

"I want you to come all over my cock. To scream my name."

"Please, Devil."

"Tell me what you need."

"I need to come."

Over and over he pounded inside her, taking what he wanted, fucking her harder than ever before, giving her exactly what she wanted, pulling her hair.

The moment her orgasm hit, he felt her clutching at him, crying his name, hungry, desperate, aching, in need.

He wanted more, so much more.

Her cunt was so tight as it milked him, wanting all of him.

Slamming inside her to the hilt, he closed his eyes, seeing stars as he pulsed deep inside her, filling her up.

Afterward, he pulled out of her and watched as his milky cum leaked from her pussy. He loved watching this. She was the perfect woman, his woman.

"Some things never change," Lexie said, looking over her shoulder at him.

"I can't help it. You always look good enough to eat to me." He gripped the back of her neck, drawing her close, pressing his lips against hers. "And I'll always be hungry for more."

****

Lexie flicked through the magazine as Devil made dinner. She sat at the kitchen counter, and he wouldn't let her cook, do the dishes, clean, or even do the laundry. Not that any laundry needed doing. They were both completely naked and had been since they arrived.

She found it so amazing to just be walking around without a care in the world.

"What do you think will happen if Simon and Tabitha actually marry?" she asked.

"They'll marry."

"But what if he decides to change to The Skulls?"

She saw his back go straight. He didn't like thinking about this, but it was something they were going to have to consider soon.

"We'll cross that path if and when we get to it."

"He's not getting any younger."

"I know that. But he still has high school, college, and, like, another ten years on top of that before he even thinks about a future."

She pressed her lips together. "You really have a problem with the whole Grandad thing, don't you?"

"I'm too young to be a Grandpa."

She laughed.

"Seriously, Lexie, stop it."

"I'm sorry. I know I shouldn't laugh, but I can't seem to help it. You're going to be one whether you like it or not. I'll be a Grandma."

"You'll be the sexiest Grandma going." He leaned over the counter and pressed a kiss to her lips. "And I'll be the best Grandpa."

"Even better than Tiny."

"He already is one, so it doesn't count."

She smiled.

"Besides, I don't see Simon giving up Chaos Bleeds, do you?" he asked.

"I don't really know what he'll do to be honest, Devil. I think about it. I kind of have to, you know. I like to be prepared for everything."

"I … wonder. I don't spend a lot of time thinking about what will happen. I wonder how it'll work out. She's a woman, so I don't see her running The Skulls. Right now, freaky little Anthony seems more suited to leading The Skulls."

"Freaky little Anthony, seriously?"

"What? The kid stares a lot and rarely talks."

"He's a kid."

"I know. We've got a lot of them, and believe me, kids talk. He doesn't. He's always staring. At times he reminds me of those kids in horror movies. You know the kind that seem all sweet and innocent but are possessed or some shit. Come and kill you while you sleep, hissing, snarling, and growling."

She couldn't stop laughing. "Okay, I had no idea you felt that way."

"Kid is freaky."

"By the way, he does talk. Just not a lot. He stares mostly at Daisy as well."

"Poor girl will develop a complex."

She shook her head, turning the page to see another luxury beach house. "Are you sure you know what you're doing?" she asked, glancing over at the food.

"I do."

"Well, when you call Angel to ask her about what you're cooking, I wouldn't tell her what you think of her very loving son."

"I have no intention of doing that. Like I said, some days he freaks me out, others he doesn't."

He dialed Angel. "I need your help."

"What are we making tonight?" Angel asked.

"Chicken pasta."

"Yum."

"Hey, Angel," Lexie said.

"Lexie, how are you doing? Having fun?"

"Yep, this place is awesome. How are things?"

"Excellent. Simon is with Tabitha in the yard. Do you want me to grab him?"

"Nah, it'll be fine. I know he's okay."

"Okay."

Lexie listened as Angel gave Devil instructions, telling him exactly what to do. It was fun to watch him chop vegetables, marinate chicken, and prepare pasta. He wouldn't let her do a single thing, which was fine. She didn't mind watching him in the kitchen.

She knew when they got home, that would fall back to her.

These moments though, they were always precious to her.

After half an hour, Angel told him what to do to finish the dish, and they said their goodbyes.

Devil wiped his brow. "Fuck, coking is hard work."

She chuckled. "Imagine doing it every single day and not having the first clue what to cook."

"Have I said recently how much I love you?"

"You've mentioned it a few times."

"Well, I fucking love you and worship the ground you walk on." He cupped her face. "So, so much."

She tilted her head back, moaning as his lips captured hers.

"It's so hard cooking?" she said.

He trailed his lips down to her neck, sucking on her pulse. Closing her eyes, she arched up, moaning as his fingers teased across her nipple. She wanted him, always.

"Please," she said.

"First, dinner, and then I'll fuck you again."

Their time was going by so fast. It was the one thing she didn't like. It wouldn't be long before they were traveling home.

She watched as Devil carefully drained the pasta, and he'd even put on an apron to protect himself.

Resting her head on her hand, she watched, completely taken with him being in the kitchen. His ink was covered a little by the strings of the apron tied at the back. Not a moment went by when she didn't fall in love with him.

"I see that love in your eyes," he said, bringing the large pot of pasta to the counter. He worked the chicken and vegetables into the pasta with some cooking water, cheese, and a splash of cream.

"I find this really sexy."

"You do?"

"Yep, it's making me really wet."

"Good, because I'm going to fuck you until you're begging me to never stop."

"I like the sound of that."

He served them, and she twirled her fork in the pasta and sauce, closing her eyes as her taste buds were teased.

"This is really good."

"I'll do anything for you and to show you how much I love and appreciate everything you do."

He reached out, twirling a strand of hair around her ear.

With them being far away from the club, she smiled at him. She saw the love shining in his eyes. Again, something he reserved for her and only her.

Chapter Eight

Devil stroked Lexie's hair. Her head was resting in his lap. Like this, he felt at peace. Calm, relaxed, happy. Nothing could touch him, not yet anyway.

"This thing with the Billionaires," she said. "What does it mean? I know I was there when you agreed to it and that it sounded great at the time, but I don't even know what's going to happen."

He didn't stop stroking her hair. "The Billionaires have a mission, to save women who've been the victims of human trafficking."

"I get that. I understand that. What can Chaos Bleeds and The Skulls really do?"

"We'll be providing safe houses for the women. Protect them. Similar work to what we do for Granito."

"It'll be dangerous?" she asked.

"I imagine at times it will be, only because these men don't know when to stop. It's like they don't even realize they're fucking dead." He didn't like sex traffickers. When Gonzalez made them house women, use them in their strip club, he'd been fucking sickened. Devil recalled not being able to look in the mirror for a long time as he didn't like what he saw. It was one of the few occasions that he hated about himself. He'd been weak, and after that, he vowed to do what he could to never become someone's little messenger. "The Billionaires have reputations to protect. They don't want everyone knowing it's them, with their companies and stuff. This way, they're able to continue their work. They'll be paying for the women and girls they save. I told them it's not just women and girls they take. It's boys and men as well."

"I hate hearing about this. I know I brought it up, but it's the thought of what they go through. I was so lucky to meet Vincent that day. You know, after I lost my job."

"Yeah, I know."

"I don't imagine many bosses would have been like him."

"They're not. Vincent's a one-of-a-kind man." He fanned her hair out. "I'll never put you in any danger. The Billionaires will have means and ways of keeping us all safe. That I have no doubt. This isn't a part-time cause for them." He actually had respect for them for reaching out, knowing the scale of human trafficking was so big that they couldn't handle it themselves.

"I want to help. Any way I can. They'll need clothes, and we'll need to help them get their lives back."

"It's going to be hard. I don't want our kids around, and we're already working on a safe house as well. We won't be having them at the clubhouse."

"Isn't that risky?"

"Not as risky as having them at the clubhouse. I got this all worked out and settled."

"I know you do." She kissed his thigh.

"So, the whole Simon and Tabitha thing," he said.

She smiled, and he saw the humor in her eyes.

"You don't need to smirk like that," he said.

"You've been thinking about it."

"Of course I have. I've not been married to you this long without knowing for a fact you're going to want me to think about it. If Simon and Tabitha were to get married, I would love for her to join Chaos Bleeds. She'll always have a home here. Any of The Skulls would have a home here."

"But, what if it goes the other way?"

"If Simon wants to become a Skull, I will accept it."

"What about a merger of the two clubs?" she

asked.

To this, he sighed.

"Still a pain for you?"

"Yeah. We're two different clubs, and I don't want to lose mine because he wants to be with a girl."

"Devil? None of you would lose the club. You'd just be ... together. It's no different than what you are now. Maybe change it to a new name for yourself."

"How about we put that on the back burner of conversation and we talk about something else?" he asked.

She chuckled. "I think it's so cute how you get so wrapped up in these things."

"I can't help it. The Skulls and Chaos Bleeds, we've been fighting together for so long. We've got a lot of history together. I don't know. I guess I'm not ready to share that kind of responsibility."

"Like you said, we've got a long time to wait for that to happen. You never know what the future holds."

"I'm hoping my son keeps it in his pants."

She wrinkled her nose. "I don't like thinking about our kids having sex, or anything like that. Having kids is a lot of hard work, not to mention commitment. If neither of them is ready for that, then they're screwed."

"Tabitha won't let that happen," he said.

"How do you know?"

"She's got her head stuck on straight. Eva's a good mother to her. Then of course she's got Tate by her side. I don't see an unplanned pregnancy in our future." He really fucking hoped it wouldn't be in his future.

Lexie sat up and crawled across the sofa, straddling his lap. "You have a way with words, you know that?"

"I do. I love rolling them together. You know, making sentences and stuff."

She chuckled. "I love you so damn much." She pressed her lips against his.

"You know, if I'd not gotten the snip, you'd totally be knocked up by now."

"Then you go and ruin it with words like that," she said.

Lexie didn't move off his lap though.

"How about I show you some of my other skills? The kind that will get you pregnant just by being in the same room as me."

He made her laugh once again, and he couldn't help but join her. This had to be the best anniversary ever. He was even thankful he'd forgotten their first one because he knew deep in his heart, he'd remember this for the rest of his life.

****

"Do you think we should ever tell him about Kayla?" Lexie asked.

Devil paused in stroking her arm. Kayla was always a topic that they didn't agree on.

"No."

"He has a right to know," she said.

Every time he called her mom, she felt a little twang of guilt that he didn't know the truth. Over the years, she'd always come back to it.

"She dumped him in your arms and left. Kayla didn't give a fuck about him and wouldn't have ever returned."

"It doesn't change the fact that she's still his mom, you know. He needs to know."

"I don't think so. It'll confuse him. You're his mother, Lexie. She's not even alive. So you'd be telling him about his *dead* mother. A title she had no right to claim either."

They lay in bed, snuggled up together after

another day of running around the island. Devil had picked her up, carrying her a few feet out to the ocean, and each time, she freaked. There could be sharks there.

He tilted her head back, and she looked up at him. "I know you don't want to hurt him. I don't either. What good would it do for him to know the truth?"

"I don't know. I can't help but worry that one day he's going to be angry with us about this."

"He won't find out, so there's no need to worry."

"You promise?"

"Cross my heart." He leaned down, pressing a kiss to her lips. "I need you to stop worrying about this."

"You do?"

"Yes."

She sighed. "I love you, Devil. I just don't want anything to hurt us."

"It won't, baby," he said. "I won't let it."

She cupped his face and kissed his lips.

Devil broke the kiss to move behind her, his body flush against hers. She moaned as he began to run his hands all over her back. The moment he touched her, all fear and doubt fled as he began to build her arousal.

Slowly, he caressed down her body before moving up.

His fingers teased, making her ache and want him again and again. When he grabbed a pillow and placed it beneath her hips, she knew what was coming.

Devil spread the cheeks of her ass, his fingers stroking across her anus. She closed her eyes, giving herself over to him and the pleasure.

He slid his fingers into her pussy only to bring them back, coating her in her own arousal.

He pressed a finger within her ass, and she gasped. No matter how many times they did this, there was always a burn, a pinch, just a little pain that made her ache for more.

With his other hand, he teased her clit, plunging fingers inside her pussy before touching her clit.

"Do you want my dick inside this juicy ass?"

"Yes."

"Ask me."

"Fuck my ass, Devil, please."

He groaned, and his teeth grazed her shoulder. She gasped, whimpering as he continued to work her ass, slipping a finger to the knuckle inside her, then a second finger, stretching her out.

"I'm going to put my dick inside you now."

She nodded her consent. She wanted it.

The large, bulbous head pressed to her pussy, and he slid inside, coating himself once again. He moved the tip to her ass, and she gasped as he pushed past those muscles, filling her inch by inch.

"Oh, fuck," they both said together.

It had been a long time, and she'd forgotten how much she loved him doing this to her. The pleasure and pain combined together, and every single part of her seemed completely on edge, tense, waiting for more.

"Please, please," she said.

"Play with your pussy," he said. "I want you to come."

In and out, he slid inside her, and she stroked her pussy, bringing herself close to orgasm.

Devil held her hips and fucked her, taking his sweet time, creating that burn she loved so much. She didn't stay quiet as he took her.

She screamed his name, begged him not to stop, and was so desperate for more she couldn't control herself.

"Please, please," she said.

"Come for me, Lexie. Let me feel how fucking

hot you are for my dick inside your ass."

When she came, she came hard. Devil let her have it. He took her to new heights, making up for lost time, driving in deep. When he came, she felt every single pulse and jet of his orgasm flooding her ass.

He didn't pull out of her. He wrapped his arms around her, holding her close.

"I don't want to go home," he said. "I want to stay with you right here forever. Make love to you, run on the beach naked."

"Home is where we need to be."

"I know."

He kissed her neck, shoulder, and simply held her.

This was her man. The one she loved. Nothing and no one was going to take that away from her.

She loved him more than anything in the world.

"Happy Anniversary, Lexie," he said. "You mean the world to me."

She smiled and then moaned as he pulled out of her ass. Within seconds he had her in his arms, and he was leading her toward the bathroom.

He loved doing this, she knew he did. Cleaning her, helping her to soak in the tub so she'd relax and wouldn't hurt.

They'd been married for a long time now, and she knew even if they were married for fifty years or a hundred, there would never be enough time.

Their love wasn't something that was bound by their time together living. She'd met her soul mate in Devil, and he'd found his in her.

****

Back at home, Devil opened up all the windows and the doors leading out to the yard. They'd only just arrived, and they'd be getting their kids tomorrow. He'd be driving down to Fort Wills with the family, where they'd have a meal before heading back.

Wrapping his arm around his wife as she stood in the yard, he kissed her neck. "Happy to be home?"

"Yes and no."

He could have gladly stayed on that island for the rest of his life.

"Tell me it'll always be like this? Promise me?"

"I promise, baby. You'll always be my number one, and I will love you, honor you, cherish you, and be faithful to you. You've got me by the balls, darlin'. The only person who doesn't always see it is you."

He kissed her neck, and she held him tightly.

Together, exactly as they were supposed to be.

Chapter Nine

Simon and Tabitha Extra

"We should head back," Tabitha said. She shoved her hands into her jeans, staring up at Simon. He'd come calling for her, and she'd wanted to go out, even though her parents didn't want her to. She couldn't stay at home right now.

Everything felt like a trap.

They were trying to confine her into one room, to make her talk about her feelings or to deal with stuff, and she couldn't handle that.

"We can head back if you want."

She nibbled her lip, frowning as she did. Why was he giving in so easily?

"I don't know."

"Tabby, I'm here for you. You just got to ask for it, and I'll give it to you."

He didn't have to come and call for her. He'd been spending time with Anthony, which was just fun to think about. Anthony loved silence. It's why they got along so well. She didn't mind his lack of talking. They often spent hours in the same room without saying a single word.

"I just want to be able to forget for a few hours. Can you help me do that? To just think about something else."

He nodded, taking her hand. "Let's keep walking."

She held onto him as he led her further through the woods. They'd been here many times when he visited in the past. Not when they were really young, but with everything going on with Darcy, not a lot of parents were paying them much mind.

Simon gripped her hand tightly, helping her over a large boulder as they walked into the clearing of the large meadow. In the spring, bluebells covered the grass for miles, and she loved to walk through it, running her hands across the grass.

"She's going to be okay," Simon said, pulling her into his arms.

She sighed. "Don't say stuff like that. Only time will tell if she's fine. Besides, you're supposed to be helping me. Not reminding me why it hurts so much."

He ran his hands up and down her back, and she held him close.

"Relax." He pulled away, and she watched as he removed his jacket. He didn't have a leather one just yet, so he always wore his denim one. "Come and sit with me."

Sitting on her butt, she lay back on his jacket, which he bundled up for their heads to rest on.

She stared up at the sky. It was so clear and blue. She loved doing this with him. Just lying together. He held her hand, and everything felt calm inside her.

"You'll get through this," he said. "And I'll be here for you always."

"What about when you go back to Piston County? What then?"

"I'll always be here for you. That will never change."

He was so good to her. Whenever she called him, he was there to answer, no matter the time of day or night.

"I miss you when you leave."

"I miss you too."

"I don't ever want you to go. It gets really hard to see you disappear."

He stroked her cheek. "One day we'll be together

forever."

She smiled. She never doubted a single word he said.

"I heard you got suspended from school?"

"Yeah, I did."

"How?"

"I broke a guy's nose using that sucker punch you showed me." She held up her hand that still had some bruising on it.

"Why?"

"He pinched Daisy's butt and told her that for a fat chick she had a nice ass. He thought that would be the end of it. I saw how upset she was, and I just reacted. I don't like anyone bullying my friends. I'm a Skull. So, I broke his nose."

She saw the laughter in Simon's eyes. "I can't believe you did that."

"I did. Daisy was mortified."

"I'm surprised Miles or Anthony didn't take care of it."

"Oh, Anthony did. He broke the guy's wrist. Told him he had to learn some manners."

"But Anthony's still in school?"

"Yep. He did the damage away from public view. He came home a few days after I got suspended, told me what he did. Told me next time, to let him deal with it." She shrugged. "That's not going to happen. I saw the look on Daisy's face. She hated it."

"I wish I could have been there."

"To beat him up?"

"Nah, to see you beat him up. I bet you looked hot."

She chuckled. "Seriously?"

"Well, yeah. I know never to take you on in a fight, but it's funny to watch other guys try to beat you."

"I've always got my friends' backs. Daisy needs it. She doesn't seem to have what it takes to, you know, fight."

"I don't know, she has got some serious 'tude. She gives me the bitch vibe."

"She's going through a lot of stuff right now."

"Like what?" Simon asked. "You're the same age as her and not a bitch."

"I can't tell you."

"Why not?"

"Because we're besties and Daisy doesn't want anyone else to know."

"Besties? I'm your soul mate."

She laughed. "You can't tell another living soul."

"I won't."

"She started her period. You know, the flow and stuff."

"Yeah, I know what that is."

"It makes her cranky, and then she's been in touch with her dad. You know, her real one, and that sucks. He didn't even fight for her or anything when we were a lot younger. Then this stuff with Darcy, and yeah, it gets to her."

"You started your period, and you don't act like a bitch."

"You don't see me every second of every day. Believe me, I've got a mean streak." She sat up, unfolding his denim jacket and putting her arms through. "How do I look?" She got to her feet and turned left then right, pouting as she'd seen some of the women on the catwalk do.

"Beautiful."

She grabbed his hands and pulled him up.

"Well, well, well, what do we have here?"

Tabitha turned to see it was Luke and Ryan. They

all went to the same school, but they were part of a rival MC group who lived in the next town over. Since the change had brought two schools together, The Skulls now went to school with them. She didn't know which one spoke, nor did she care.

"Well, if it's not little Tabitha. Where's your twin?" Ryan asked.

"Why would I need Miles?" she asked. "I was quite happy to rearrange your face without him. Simon, this is the reason I was suspended from school. It seems he can't handle being beaten up by a girl. I like to think of him as Dickface."

Dickface Ryan still had bruises around his eyes, and his nose patched up. Anthony's handiwork was still there with his hand still wrapped up.

She wasn't afraid of them even if they did try to intimidate her. Luke wasn't so bad, but Dickface tried to scare her off and she wasn't having any of it.

Every now and then he found her alone in high school, and those times he'd tried to make her uncomfortable. She hadn't told anyone about him as a quick kick between his thighs backed him the fuck off.

"And there is Asshole, also known as Luke."

"I see you think you're tough when you got a boy to protect you," Dickface said.

"I don't need a boy for anything. I can fight my own battles. What about you? Need someone to come and hold your hand?"

"Are we having any trouble here?" Anthony said, stepping out of the clearing. His arms were folded, and he looked fucking pissed off. Miles was beside him, and both looked fucking angry.

Dickface paled, and she found that so funny. She winked at him, and he took a step back. This was why she refused to back down to him.

Beneath all his façade he was a fucking a coward.

"No trouble. Just out walking."

"You're in Fort Wills. That means you're trespassing," Anthony said.

Luke pointed at a line. "I believe this is the border line. We're not trespassing on anyone's land." He turned his gaze to her. "You should think about that."

She took Simon's hand, no longer interested in staying.

"See you around," Luke said.

She walked up to Anthony and her brother.

"What's the big deal?" Tabitha asked.

"Parents were looking for you," Miles said. "They've got dinner ready. I told them you just needed to clear your head and I'd come and get you."

"Shoot, I forgot."

"What was going on here?" Miles asked.

"We just came to relax when those two showed up," she said, pushing some hair off her face.

"Who are they?" Simon asked.

"They're the guys I've told you about in all my letters. It's nothing for you to worry about, I promise."

"We got a handle on it," Anthony said.

"Parents don't like it though," Miles said. "I've heard talk they want a meet to make sure they know to stay the hell away from us."

"They don't scare me." Anthony glared in their direction.

Glancing over her shoulder, she saw the two were still talking. Luke stared at her, and she quickly looked back at Anthony.

"You look like you want to hurt them."

"I do, Tab. I do. You can't come here alone. I don't trust them."

"Please, you're the one that likes to play with

knives," she said. She'd caught him many times playing with his mother's collection.

He raised a brow. "You want to go there?" he asked.

She shook her head. "I'm getting hungry."

"Simon, you've got to come back with us."

"Ugh, I'll talk to you later," Simon said. He pulled her in close and kissed her head.

They headed out of the woods, and while Anthony and Simon went one direction, she and Miles went the other.

He was her twin, but they were complete opposites.

He was the more levelheaded of the two of them, whereas she had to control her temper most of the time.

"You shouldn't be alone when you go to the meadow."

"I get that. Anthony just said it."

"But I know you only hear what you want to hear," Miles said. "Those guys are bad news."

"I can take care of myself."

"I know you're strong, but we're not stupid either."

She was always angry when people treated them like kids. They were not kids and hadn't been for a long time. Their lives in the club made that clear.

"Don't put yourself at risk when you don't need to. I wouldn't want anything to happen to you. If they did something, it would start a war between the clubs, Tab. You're my sister, and I don't want to lose you."

"You really think Dickface and Asshole are that big of a threat."

"Not so much Asshole but Dickface, he's a problem. I know you don't talk about it, but I'm sure you've seen him around school. The way he is."

She didn't say anything as she didn't want Miles to worry. "I'll be careful. Not going to the meadow without someone."

"Good. Now let's go and eat."

****

"If you're not back by six, I'm throwing you to the wolves," Anthony said.

Simon stood on the window ledge. "I get it. I get it. Thanks for doing this, man. I appreciate it."

"I'm not doing this for you. I'm doing it for Tabitha."

"I didn't like those guys out at the meadow today."

Anthony shrugged. "That's not my problem. It's part of the school, and you can't do anything about it."

"Do you know if any of them are giving Tabitha trouble?"

"Dude, she broke a guy's nose because he touched Daisy. It's made her public enemy number one. She doesn't have a problem with that. I wish I was there to see what he did."

"Why wait to take him on?" Simon asked.

"My dad will be pissed if I got suspended. Mom already wanted me to go and see a shrink when I was a kid. She thinks something's wrong with my head."

"I always did think you were weird," Simon said.

"Do you want help or not? I can shout for them right now. Dad will lock you in a different room. You won't be able to go and see Tabitha for a long time."

"Screw you."

"Are we done? You talk too much, and I'm bored."

"You got porn to watch or something?"

"Get out."

Anthony closed the window, and Simon didn't

linger. He and Anthony would never see eye to eye, but that was more than okay. He wasn't interested in him. Out of all The Skulls, he and Anthony put up with each other because of their friends. Climbing down the tree he was careful as he passed the kitchen window where Lash and Angel were talking. Once he passed the yard, he ran down the street and headed straight for Tiny and Eva's house.

If his father caught him now, Devil would make him pay. He shouldn't be climbing into a girl's window. He was leaving tomorrow, and he didn't want to waste another moment of it. His dad would be pissed. He'd been asked to be a good kid while they'd been away, and he had been. Instead of sticking by Tabitha's side or wandering the streets, he'd stayed close to Anthony, and that guy was a buzzkill on a grand scale. He didn't do anything fun.

Tabitha had also been too busy with Darcy, and he didn't want to come between the two. Taking her to the meadow today was the first time they'd gotten together.

Thinking about the meadow, of holding her in his arms, he didn't want to let her go. The meadow brought up memories of those two assholes. He didn't like the way they looked at her. Both of them clearly liked what they saw when staring at Tabitha, even if there was a bit of hate there as well.

She belonged to him, and had since they were kids.

There was no Prospect waiting around to stop him, so he moved toward the side of the house where her bedroom was. He started the climb, being careful not to bang the side of the house or make too much noise to alert her parents.

"What are you doing?" Tabitha asked.

He was surprised to see her sitting at the window with her legs hanging out. She looked like she didn't have a single care in the world.

"What are you doing?"

"This is my bedroom."

"You know you could fall and break your neck."

"Like you could right now. You're climbing up the side of my house. What if the window had been locked?" she asked. "You wouldn't have had anywhere to go."

"I wanted to see you. Dad's coming back tomorrow to pick me up, and I'm not ready to say goodbye to you yet. If you want me to go, I can leave."

"I don't want you to leave. We haven't spent a whole lot of time together."

She smiled, and he saw she was wearing his denim jacket. She climbed back inside her window and held it open, helping him climb through.

"Phew, I didn't think you were going to help me there."

"You've got to keep your voice down." She rushed over to her door, and he waited as she closed it gently.

Her light was already turned off.

She wore a pair of pajamas underneath his jacket.

"You're staying the night?"

"Yeah, Anthony's covering for me, you know. So I wanted to come and spend some time with you."

"It's not like Anthony. He must really want you out of his room." She moved up to him and hugged him tight. "I feel like I didn't get to see you much this visit. I'm so pleased you came."

"You've been busy, but all you need to do is ask and I'll be here, always." If he hadn't come to Fort Wills, he'd have ended up staying with Ripper and Judi, and that would not do, not for him.

She pulled away, and he watched as she covered a yawn.

"You want to get into bed?" he asked.

Tabitha nodded.

She pulled up the covers, sliding beneath.

He joined her on top, putting his arm around her. She snuggled against his side and sighed.

"I don't like those guys being near you."

"You've got nothing to worry about. I know how to take care of myself."

"I know, but you shouldn't be fighting them. What if they hurt you?"

"It'll be fine. You've got to stop worrying." She tilted her head back, and he once again saw the sadness in her eyes.

"I worry a lot about you. You know, with all the changes and stuff. You going to a new school and now those guys are there."

"I get it. I do. I don't like it. I know my parents don't like it either."

"Do you have classes with them?"

"A couple of them, but for the most part we stay out of each other's way. It's easier that way. The first day we all got into a fight. We were all pulled into the principal's office. They started it. We just finished it."

He didn't like that, but knowing she had Miles and Anthony at least, he knew she would be fine.

"You don't have to worry."

"It's going to be okay."

"I know."

"I'm not talking about those guys or the school."

"I know." She didn't believe him.

"You know, you could just convince your dad to move to Piston County," he said.

She chuckled. "Like that is ever going to happen."

"You know they're friends now. It could happen."

"Yeah, I don't see that happening at all. Could you imagine my dad with a Chaos Bleeds cut?"

"My dad would totally make him earn that patch," Simon said. "It'll be fun to watch."

"What will happen if you find someone else?" she asked, changing conversation. This was one of the reasons why Simon knew he'd never get bored with her. She was always going off on a tangent, and he had to keep up with what she was talking about.

"Someone else?"

"Someone better than me. I'm a Skull, Simon. We're two different clubs. I know how it works."

"You mean another girl?" he asked.

"Yes."

He laughed. There was nothing else he could do. "There won't ever be anyone better than you." He took her hand, placing it against his chest. "You own my heart." Staring at where her hand lay on his chest, he felt himself calm down. She always had this effect on him, even as a kid. "That sounded really cheesy."

"A little bit but I love cheesy," she said.

They both started giggling, the noise getting louder with every passing second.

Tabitha grabbed a pillow and pressed it against his face. "Shh, we have to be quiet." She whispered the word, trying to get him to be silent. The last thing he wanted was to get caught.

"Tabitha, honey, you okay?"

Her door started to open, and Simon dropped from the bed to the floor, rolling beneath it. The space was rather tight and cramped, but he could handle it.

"Mom, what is it? What's wrong?"

He heard the nerves in Tabitha's voice. They couldn't get caught, but he didn't want to leave her, even though there would be hell to pay if anyone caught them. Their parents tolerated their relationship with each other, but at any point they wished, it could all end in disaster. He couldn't live without her. Being young was a pain in the ass because most times, they thought it was cute. This wasn't about being cute.

He loved Tabitha and had for a long time.

Ignoring his thoughts, he listened to Eva. She sat on the edge of the bed, and he hoped she didn't try to look underneath.

"Nothing's wrong. I just wanted to come and see you. Miles told us that you saw those boys today. The one whose nose you broke."

"I told you I'm not going to apologize to him. I don't care what the principal says. He pinched Daisy's ass."

"I know, honey, and watch your language."

"I'm sorry. You know Daisy doesn't defend herself. She's not good at doing stuff like that, and I don't mind it. She's my best friend."

"I know, honey, but you should have reported him to the teacher."

"They don't do anything. It's like it's one big joke to them."

"I'm sure it's not."

"Whatever," Tabitha said.

"Anyway, I was thinking we could do a girly weekend this week. Just us girls, what do you think?"

"I'd like that. Can we get some ice cream, invite Daisy over, and make it an all-girls' night? I'd like that."

"We can do that. It's been a long time since we had some fun together."

Tabitha yawned. "I'm so sorry, Mom, I'm so tired. It's been a long day."

"Okay. Get some sleep. I love you, honey."

"Love you too."

He stayed beneath the bed, hearing the door close, and only when he heard the sound of footsteps walking away did he move out from under the bed.

"I thought we were totally going to get caught," Tabitha whispered.

"Does she always come and see you at night?"

"Not until recently with Darcy. I think it has scared her, you know."

"Yeah, I know."

"I can't even begin to think what Darcy must be thinking or feeling. She tries to keep her spirits up when everyone is around, but I overheard Ink talking the other day. She cries herself to sleep when she doesn't think anyone's watching." He saw Tabitha had tears in her eyes. "I wish I could help her."

"You are helping her. By just being you, you're helping."

Silence fell between then, and he stared into her eyes, knowing there's nowhere else he'd rather be than with her. She was everything to him.

It always annoyed him when his dad or mom would give him that look as if he didn't know what love was or even understand it. He understood a whole lot, and he didn't need them to tell him what he felt. He knew what it was, and he knew what he wanted. He wanted Tabitha to be his wife more than anything.

He saw the way his dad looked at his mom, and he felt that way each time he was with Tabitha. No one could come between that.

"I do feel really tired," she said, pressing the back of her hand to her mouth, yawning.

"Go to sleep."

"I don't want you to leave without saying goodbye."

"I'll have to leave in the morning."

"That's fine. I'll be here, and I'll make sure you wake up in time."

Tabitha rested against him, and Simon stared up at the ceiling. After a few moments, he fell asleep.

The End

www.samcrescent.com

SAM CRESCENT

EVERNIGHT PUBLISHING ®

www.evernightpublishing.com

www.ingramcontent.com/pod-product-compliance
Lightning Source LLC
Chambersburg PA
CBHW020142150626
46552CB00021B/1266